TROUBLE WITH TROLLS

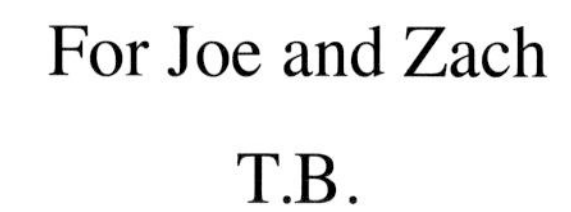

For Joe and Zach

T.B.

For Arthur. J.H. Cherrington
Our own little viking hero

G.C.

EGMONT
We bring stories to life

Book Band: White

Lexile® measure: 680L

First published in Great Britain 2018
This Reading Ladder edition published 2018
by Egmont UK Limited
The Yellow Building, 1 Nicholas Road, London W11 4AN

ISBN 978 1 4052 8683 1
www.egmont.co.uk
A CIP catalogue record for this title is available from the British Library.
Printed in Singapore
67210/1

Series consultant: Nikki Gamble

CONTENTS

Tony Bradman

Illustrated by Gary Cherrington

Reading Ladder

TEETH LIKE JAGGED ROCKS

Far away in the cold and icy North, in the Land of the Vikings, a little village lay beneath a silvery moon. The wind chased snowflakes round the houses, and all was quiet. Although something was stirring in the forest nearby . . .

In one of the houses, a boy called Erik snuggled down beneath the thick furs on his bed. It was good to be tucked up in the warm by the hearth-fire. His mother and father and his baby sister, Helga, were in their beds, snoring away.

Suddenly Erik heard some strange noises outside – THUD . . . THUD . . . THUD. The floor shook with each heavy THUD, and things fell from the shelves. Now there were more noises. It sounded like people running and yelling and screaming.

Erik sat up, just as the roof of his house was torn off with a

RRRRRRIIIIPPPPP!

An enormous, ugly head poked its way in and looked around.

A troll! The creature grinned at Erik, his giant mouth full of grey and black teeth like jagged rocks.

'PEEKABOO!' he roared. 'Got anything tasty to eat?'

Then he stuck his huge grubby hand into the house, smashing everything in his search for food. Erik's father quickly picked up Helga, who was crying. Erik's mother grabbed an axe to defend them, but the troll just ignored her.

'Quick, make for the door!' yelled Erik's father. 'We'll be safer outside.'

But they weren't safer. Two more trolls were stomping through the village. They were ripping off roofs too and trampling on everything with their huge feet. They snatched all the food they could find, and chased the sheep and goats and chickens.

The villagers tried to fight them, but it was impossible. The trolls simply knocked them over like skittles. It was a game the trolls seemed happy to play for ages . . . But eventually they decided they'd had enough fun, and turned to go.

'Well, good to meet you,' said the troll who had ripped the roof off Erik's house. 'My name is Gorm, by the way, and these are my brothers Drekk and Balgor. We rather like this place, so you can be sure we'll be back . . . soon.'

The trio of terrible trolls strolled off, their arms round each other, leaving total mayhem behind them. Poor little Helga was sobbing her tiny heart out.

Erik glared at the trolls, his heart full of anger.

JUST A BOY

In the morning, the Chief Viking of the village called a meeting. Everyone gathered in the Great Hall. Erik sat with his family, shivering in the cold. The roof had been ripped off the Great Hall as well, and that made Erik feel even worse.

He loved the Great Hall. It was the place where everyone gathered in the evenings to tell the old stories of Gods and monsters and the great heroes of the past.

'What are we going to do, Chief?' asked Erik's mother. 'Getting through the winter will be hard enough without a bunch of trolls eating all our food!'

'Yes, we'll starve!' several others called out. 'We won't last till spring!'

'We'll just have to fight them,' said Erik's father. 'They took us by surprise last night, but I'm sure we can do better next time. We're Vikings, aren't we?'

'Umm, we can try, I suppose,' said the chief. 'But trolls are pretty tough. In fact, as far as I've heard tell, they're not scared of anything.'

‘I don’t think that’s right,’ said Erik. Everyone turned to look at him. ‘I’m sure that trolls are scared of dragons. It says so in some of the old stories.’

‘But even if that’s true, how is it going to help us?’ said Erik’s mother.

‘Why don’t we find a dragon and ask it to protect us?’ said Erik.

'Seriously?' said Erik's father. 'You think the answer to our problem is a fire-breathing monster? But that would just make things even worse . . .'

Somebody disagreed with him, and an argument began. Soon everybody was yelling as loudly as they could, and poor little Helga burst into tears again.

'Who would go on such a crazy quest, anyway?' said Erik's mother at last.

Erik had tried to join in the argument, but nobody paid any attention to him. Now he stood up and spoke loudly so that he would definitely be heard.

'I'll do it,' he said. Everybody turned to stare at him once more.

'Sit down and be quiet, Erik,' said his father. 'You're just a boy.'

'Now hold on, let's not be hasty,' said

the chief. 'You're right, he is just a boy, and quite a small one, too. But if he's willing to try then I say, why not?'

'Yes, send the boy!' yelled the villagers. Erik's parents tried to argue with them, and offered to go instead of Erik, even though the whole idea was crazy. But the chief wouldn't hear of it.

'We need all the grown-ups to stay here,' he said. 'We'll dig a ditch and put up a big fence. That way we might hold off the trolls while we wait.'

So it was settled, and later that day Erik left on his quest. His parents stood at the edge of the village, watching him walk away, their faces full of worry.

'Don't worry about me,' he called out. 'I'll be fine!'

Little did he know what lay in store for him …

WICKEDLY SHARP CLAWS

It turned out that there were plenty of dragons in the Land of the Vikings. On the second day of his quest, Erik arrived at another village. The people looked unhappy, which wasn't surprising. Most of their houses had been burned down.

'Oh yes, a dragon did this,' the village chief said angrily. 'There's been a plague of them this year. If you go into the mountains you'll find them all over the place. It beats me why you'd want to, though. They're nasty, horrible creatures.'

Erik soon discovered that for himself. The village chief was right – the mountains were full of dragons.

There were big dragons, medium-sized dragons, small dragons. Some were spiky, some had scales the size of shields, some had teeth like daggers. Each one was a different colour – and they were all utterly terrifying.

They flew through the sky and perched on crags, eating sheep or preening themselves. Sometimes they fought each other. They shrieked and blasted fire and flashed their sharp claws.

Erik knew he would have to speak to them, but he had no idea how to start. At last he took a deep breath and stepped forward.

'Er . . . excuse me,' he said. 'I was wondering if I could ask you . . .'

'Can anybody hear a faint squeaking noise?' said a large dragon.

'Yes, it's coming from that irritating little creature,' said a medium-sized one.

'I believe it's a human,' said one that was small, and covered in spikes. 'What do you want, boy?'

'Well, we're having trouble with trolls in my village,' said Erik, 'and we know they're scared of dragons, so we hoped that you could come and help us.'

'Definitely not,' said the first dragon. 'We don't help humans.'

'No, we only ever eat them,' said the second, coming closer.

'Although you won't make much of a meal,' said the third.

Erik turned and ran. The dragons blasted out a wave of fire to send him on his way, and he could hear their laughter echoing off the mountains. Then he tripped and fell, and rolled head over heels down the slope until he stopped with a BUMP!

He sat up slowly, rubbing his head, and saw that he had a landed in a squelchy pile of broken branches, leaves and mud. Soon Erik realised he was sitting in a dragon's nest. It smelt awful, but it was empty apart from a lot of chewed and scorched animal bones – and a large white egg. Suddenly a crack appeared on the egg's surface.

More cracks appeared, and before long the top of the egg flew off. A strange little creature poked her head out, stared at Erik with her huge eyes, and coughed.

'Mummy!' she cheeped . . . and Erik smiled.

Lots of Frowning Faces

Erik hurried homewards and arrived the next day. The villagers spotted him coming down the track from the mountains, and everyone gathered to meet him outside the Great Hall. His parents and Helga were very pleased to see him.

‘Well then,’ said the Chief. ‘Did you manage to find a dragon?’

‘I did,’ said Erik, and the crowd murmured with excitement.

‘Really?’ said the Chief, amazed. ‘That’s wonderful! Er . . . I never doubted you for a second. So where is this marvellous creature? On its way, I suppose?’

The Chief and everyone else looked up and eagerly scanned the sky.

‘Actually, I brought her with me,’ said Erik, opening his cloak. He had been keeping the little dragon sheltered under it, and now he let her out. ‘Her name is, er . . . Astrid.’

Of course, he didn’t know her real name – but Astrid seemed right.

The crowd looked down, and the little dragon found herself surrounded by lots of frowning faces. She cheeped, then coughed, and hid behind Erik's legs.

'That's not a dragon,' said Erik's father. 'It's some kind of lizard, isn't it?'

'No, I swear she's a dragon!' said Erik. 'I saw her hatch out of an egg in a dragon's nest. I know she's a bit small, but you didn't say anything about finding a large dragon. They're all horrible, anyway. And she's bound to grow bigger.'

'I'm not sure she will,' said Erik's mother. 'She doesn't sound too good.'

She was right. Erik was quite worried about Astrid's cough, which was getting worse. Although the strange thing was that it didn't seem to bother her. She seemed just as happy as when she had first popped out of her egg.

'Even if she is a dragon, we don't have time to wait for her to grow,' said the Chief with a sigh. 'The trolls could be here any moment. We need another plan . . .'

All the shouting and yelling started once more, everybody arguing at the tops of their voices. Erik stood with the little dragon in the middle of the noise. He felt very guilty. He couldn't help thinking that he had let the village down.

Suddenly he heard a familiar noise – THUD . . . THUD . . . THUD . . .

The ground shook, and the crowd instantly fell silent. Everyone held their breath.

'Yoo-hoo, we're back!' somebody boomed. 'Have you missed us?'

'To the fence!' yelled Erik's father. 'We'll hold them there!'

But Erik could hear the fence already being smashed . . .

BIG, HORRIBLE CREATURES

The villagers had dug a very big ditch, but that didn't stop the trolls. They stepped over it, and smashed down the fence with their huge fists. Again the villagers tried to fight them off, but they were scattered like skittles just as before.

The trolls stomped through the village, ripping off the remaining roofs and grabbing whatever they fancied. Erik saw his parents trying to protect Helga, and the anger in his heart grew and grew until he just couldn't keep it in any more. He was tired of big, horrible creatures being nasty to him and the people he loved.

So he picked up his mother's axe and stood in front of the trolls.

'Leave us alone!' Erik yelled. 'Or . . . or . . . I'll chop you into pieces!'

'Oooh, look, a terrifying Viking warrior!' said Gorm. 'I'm so scared!'

All three trolls pretended to be frightened, and then they burst out laughing.

Meanwhile, Astrid's cough suddenly seemed to get even worse, if that was possible. It grew louder and louder . . . but Erik kept his eyes on the trolls.

'Run along, boy,' said Gorm at last. 'Unless you want to be squashed.'

Now Astrid's cough was almost out of control. Erik turned to look at her, and saw that something very strange was happening. Each time she coughed, a little puff of black smoke came out of her mouth – and she became a bit bigger.

The trolls were staring at her as well, their eyes wide and mouths open.

'Er . . . is that what I think it is?' muttered Drekk, his voice shaking.

'I hope not,' said Balgor, his bottom lip trembling like a baby's.

Astrid gave three final coughs – COUGH! COUGH! COUGH! – and now she wasn't a little dragon any more. She was large – and she breathed . . . FIRE!

'RUN!' screamed Gorm, and the trolls turned and fled to the forest. Astrid flew after them in hot pursuit, blasting away at them . . . and they only just made their escape. Then she flew back to the village – and everyone cheered and cheered.

It took a while to repair all the damage, but before long the village looked the same as it had done before. Of course, everyone thought Erik was a hero. They called him Dragon-Boy, and told the story in the Great Hall of how he had saved the village.

Astrid became part of Erik's family, and they all loved her, especially Helga . . .

And they were always warm in the winter.